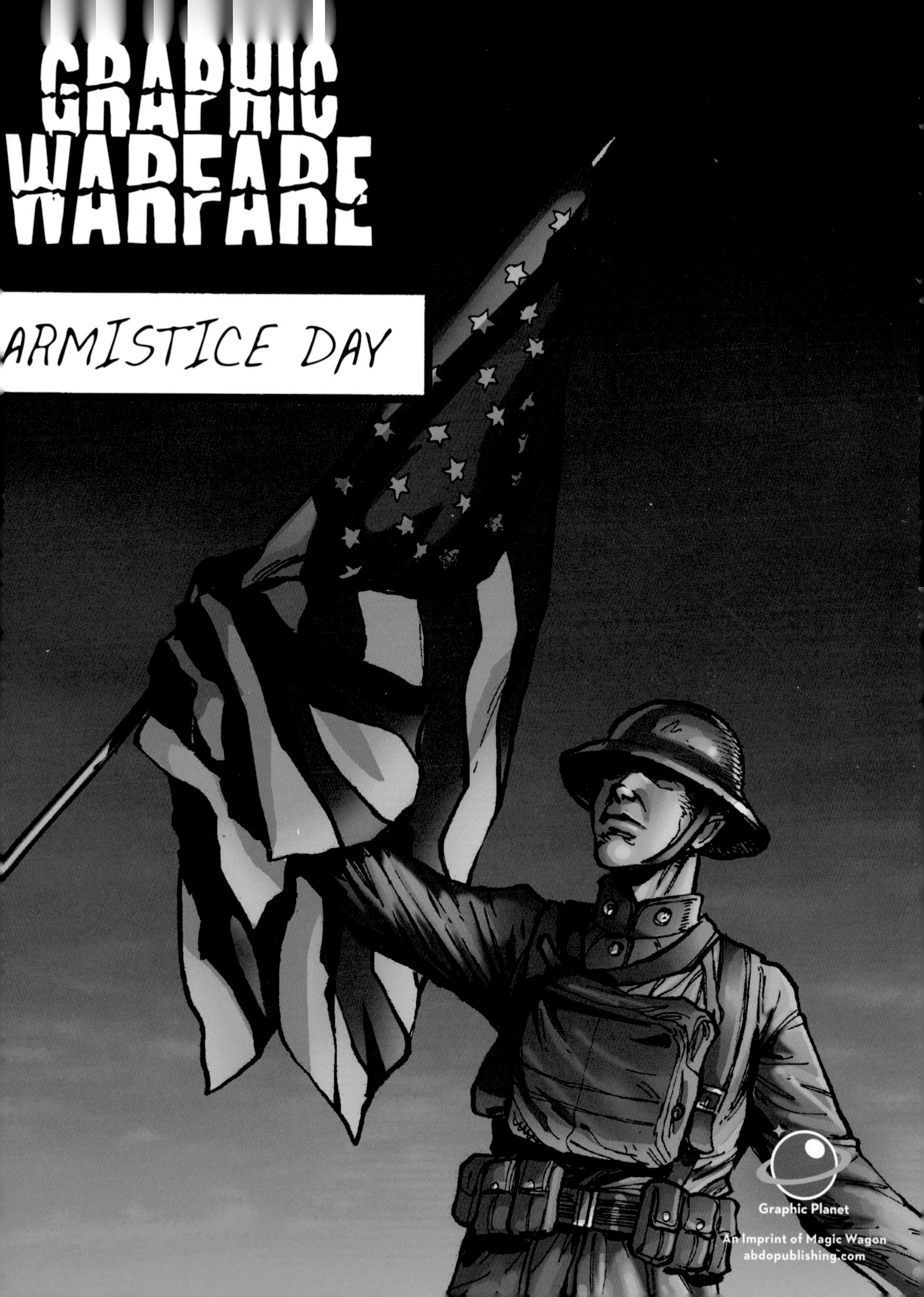
GRAPHIC WARFARE
ARMISTICE DAY
Graphic Planet
An Imprint of Magic Wagon
abdopublishing.com

ABDOPUBLISHING.COM

Published by Magic Wagon, a division of ABDO, PO Box 398166, Minneapolis, Minnesota 55439. Copyright © 2016 by Abdo Consulting Group, Inc. International copyrights reserved in all countries. No part of this book may be reproduced in any form without written permission from the publisher. Graphic Planet™ is a trademark and logo of Magic Wagon.

Printed in the United States of America, North Mankato, Minnesota.
102015
012016

Written by Joeming Dunn
Illustrated by Ben Dunn
Coloring and retouching by Robby Bevard
Lettered by Doug Dlin
Cover art by Ben Dunn
Interior layout and design by Antarctic Press
Cover design by Candice Keimig

Library of Congress Cataloging-in-Publication Data

Dunn, Joeming W.
  Armistice Day / by Joeming Dunn ; illustrated by Ben Dunn.
    pages cm. -- (Graphic warfare)
  ISBN 978-1-61641-978-3
  1. World War, 1914-1918--Comic books, strips, etc.--Juvenile literature. 2.
Armistice Day--Comic books, strips, etc.--Juvenile literature. 3. Graphic novels.
I. Dunn, Ben, illustrator. II. Title.
  D570.D86 2016
  940.4--dc23
                    2015023945

By 1918, World War I had been raging for four long years. By autumn of that year, the Allied powers had scored victories on all fronts. The Central powers had begun to surrender. German military leaders recognized that they would not win the war.

On October 4, 1918, the German government requested a cease-fire. In correspondence negotiating an armistice, President Woodrow Wilson asked for an end to submarine warfare, the retreat of Germany from all occupied lands, and a democratic government in Germany.

On November 9, Germany's Kaiser Wilhelm II abdicated and fled to the Netherlands. Two days later, representatives of France, England, and Germany met in a railroad car in the woods near Compiègne, France. There, on the eleventh hour of the eleventh day of the eleventh month, the fighting ended when they signed the Armistice of Compiègne.

In 1919, President Wilson declared November 11 to be Armistice Day. The holiday observed the end of World War I and honored its veterans. Today, it is known as Veterans Day.

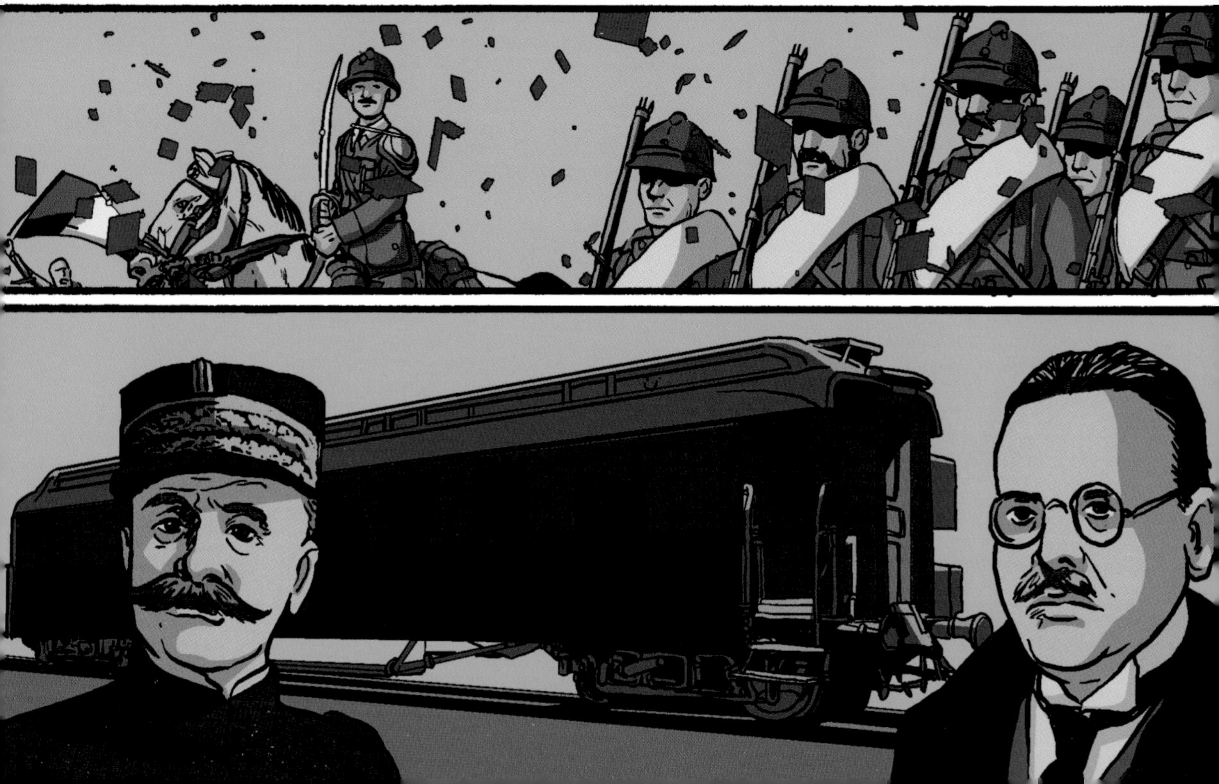

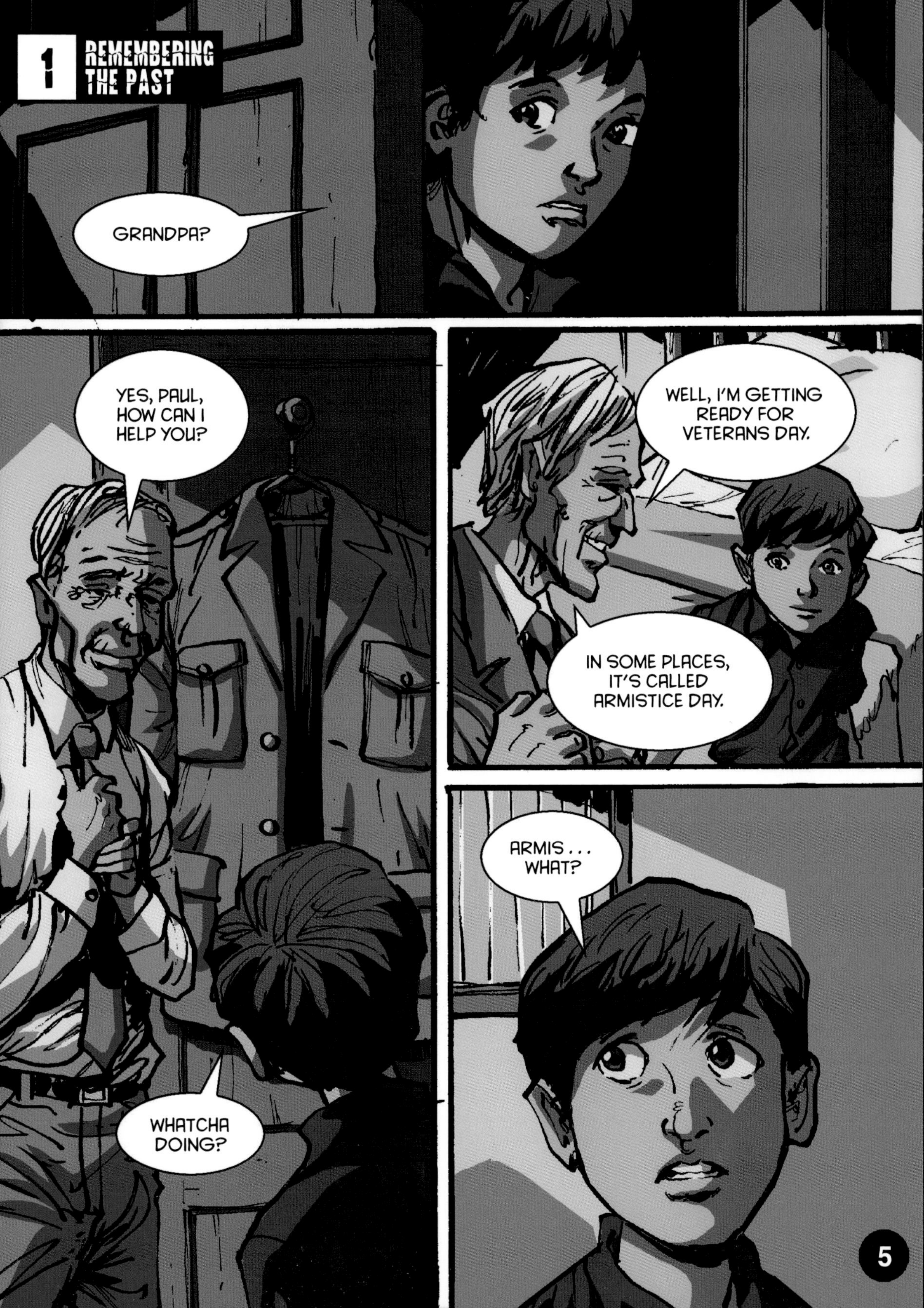
1 REMEMBERING THE PAST
GRANDPA?
YES, PAUL, HOW CAN I HELP YOU?
WHATCHA DOING?
WELL, I'M GETTING READY FOR VETERANS DAY.
IN SOME PLACES, IT'S CALLED ARMISTICE DAY.
ARMIS . . . WHAT?

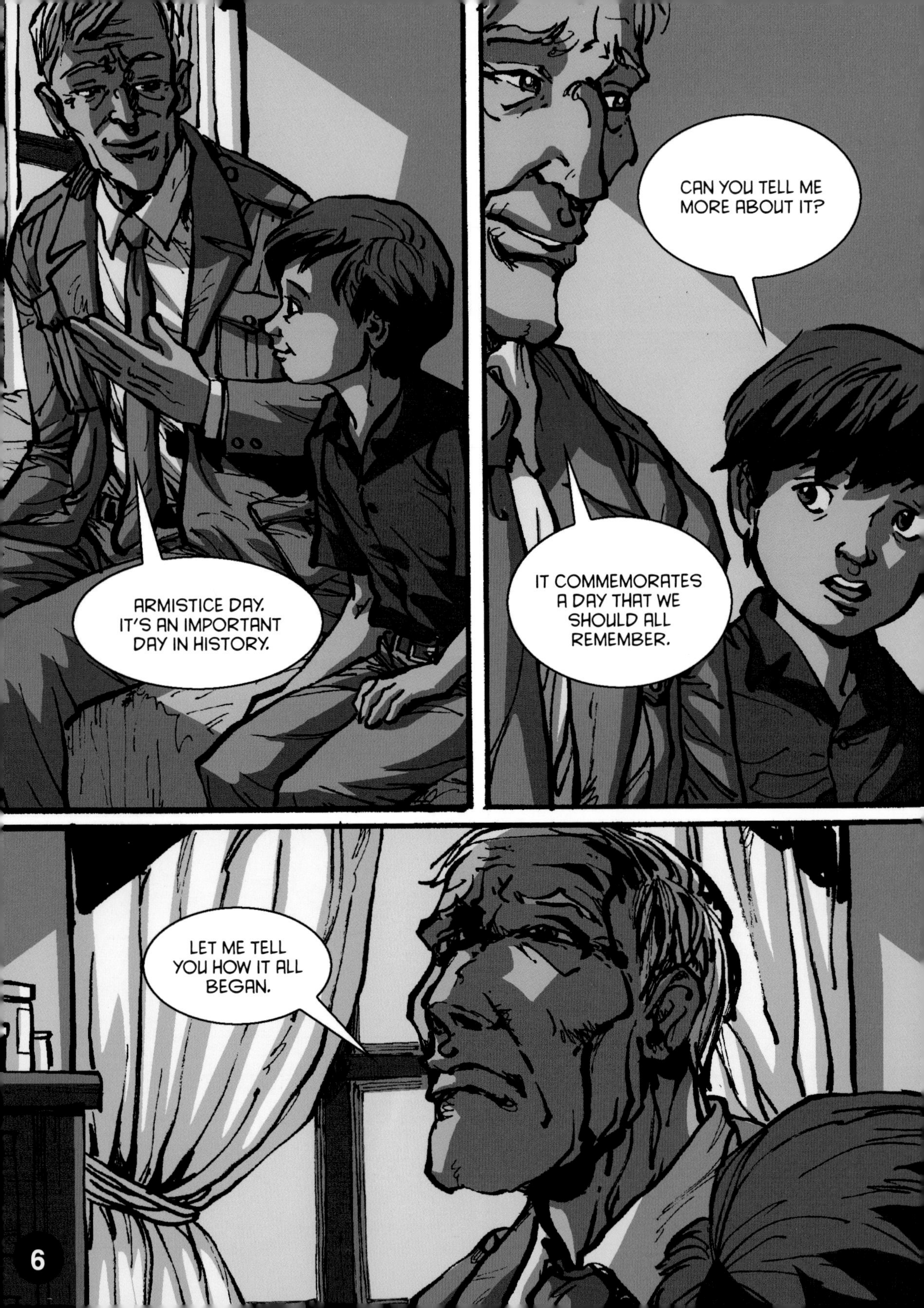
ARMISTICE DAY. IT'S AN IMPORTANT DAY IN HISTORY.
CAN YOU TELL ME MORE ABOUT IT?
IT COMMEMORATES A DAY THAT WE SHOULD ALL REMEMBER.
LET ME TELL YOU HOW IT ALL BEGAN.

2 CAUSE OF WAR

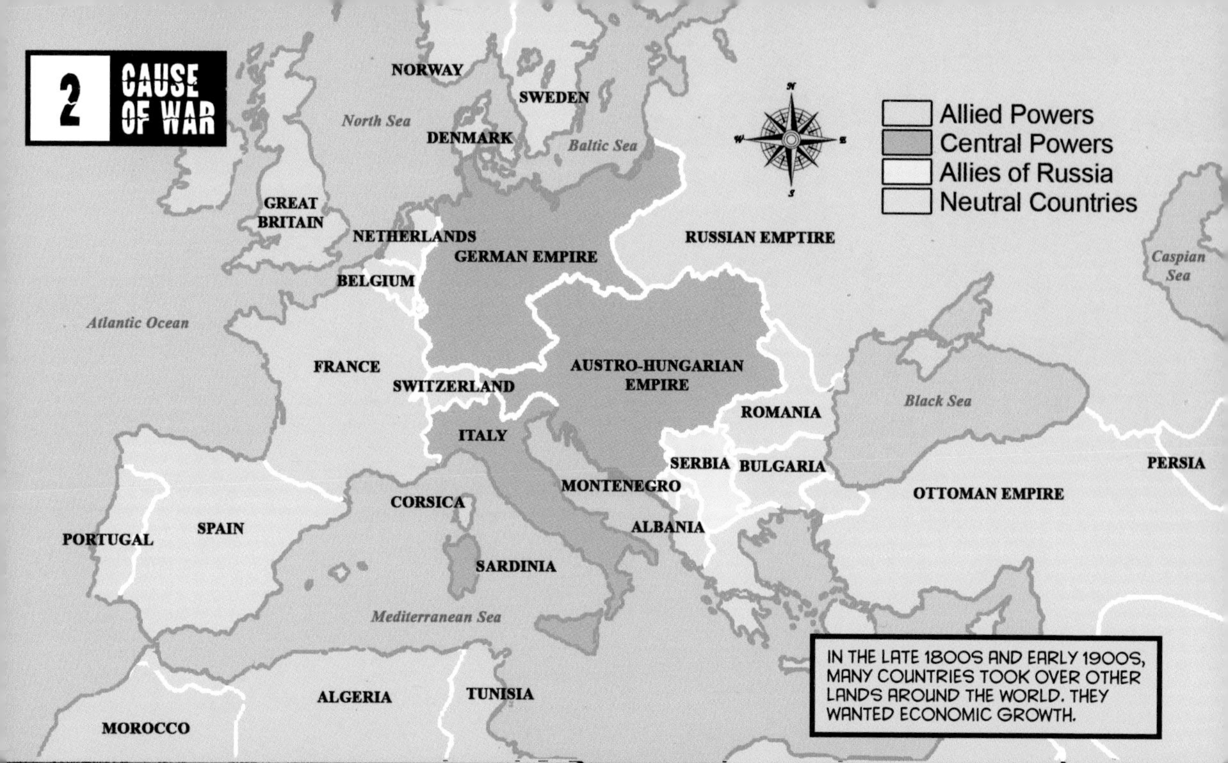

NORWAY
SWEDEN
North Sea
DENMARK
Baltic Sea
Allied Powers
Central Powers
Allies of Russia
Neutral Countries
GREAT BRITAIN
NETHERLANDS
GERMAN EMPIRE
RUSSIAN EMPTIRE
Caspian Sea
BELGIUM
Atlantic Ocean
FRANCE
SWITZERLAND
AUSTRO-HUNGARIAN EMPIRE
Black Sea
ROMANIA
ITALY
SERBIA
BULGARIA
PERSIA
MONTENEGRO
OTTOMAN EMPIRE
CORSICA
PORTUGAL
SPAIN
ALBANIA
SARDINIA
Mediterranean Sea
ALGERIA
TUNISIA
MOROCCO
IN THE LATE 1800S AND EARLY 1900S, MANY COUNTRIES TOOK OVER OTHER LANDS AROUND THE WORLD. THEY WANTED ECONOMIC GROWTH.

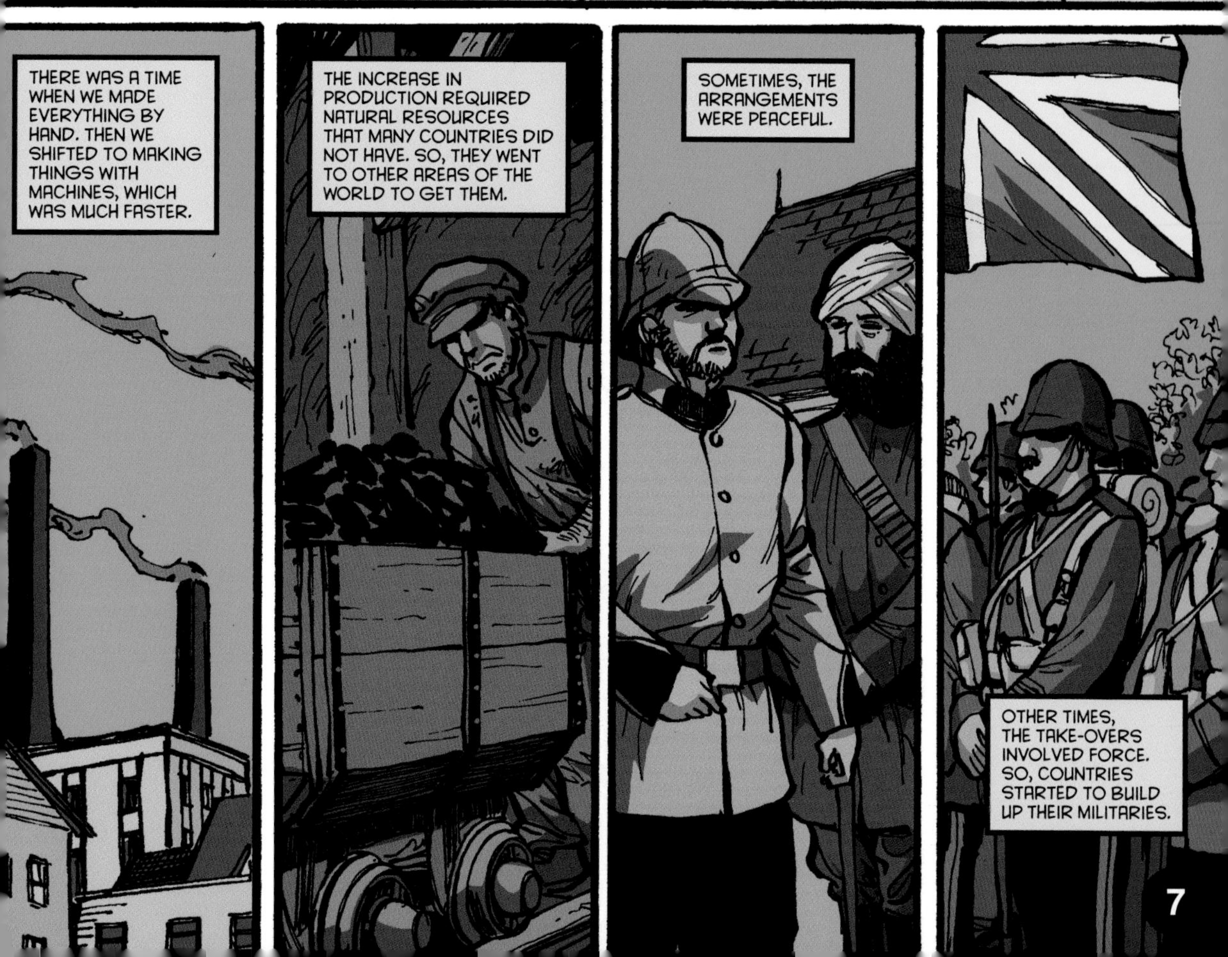

THERE WAS A TIME WHEN WE MADE EVERYTHING BY HAND. THEN WE SHIFTED TO MAKING THINGS WITH MACHINES, WHICH WAS MUCH FASTER.
THE INCREASE IN PRODUCTION REQUIRED NATURAL RESOURCES THAT MANY COUNTRIES DID NOT HAVE. SO, THEY WENT TO OTHER AREAS OF THE WORLD TO GET THEM.
SOMETIMES, THE ARRANGEMENTS WERE PEACEFUL.
OTHER TIMES, THE TAKE-OVERS INVOLVED FORCE. SO, COUNTRIES STARTED TO BUILD UP THEIR MILITARIES.

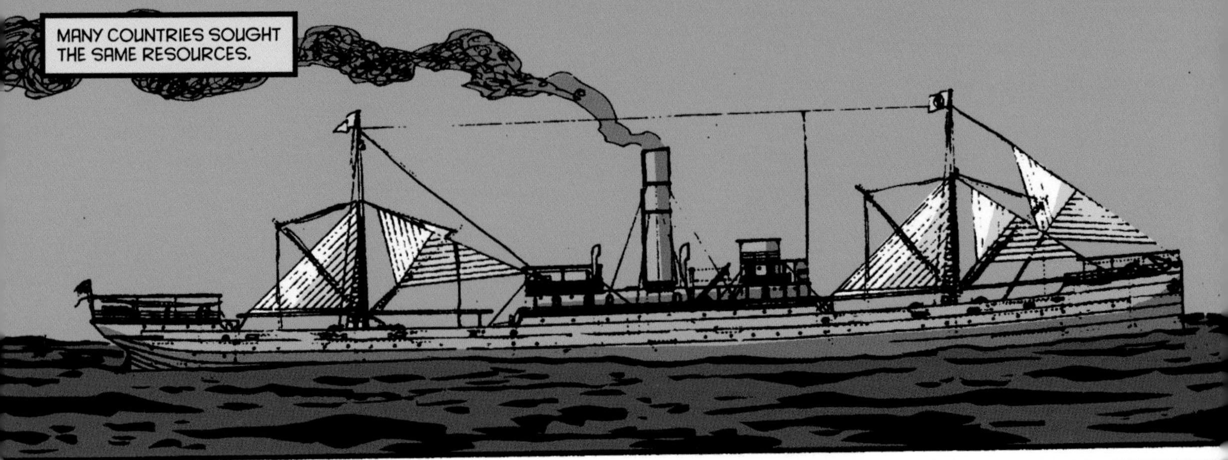
MANY COUNTRIES SOUGHT THE SAME RESOURCES.

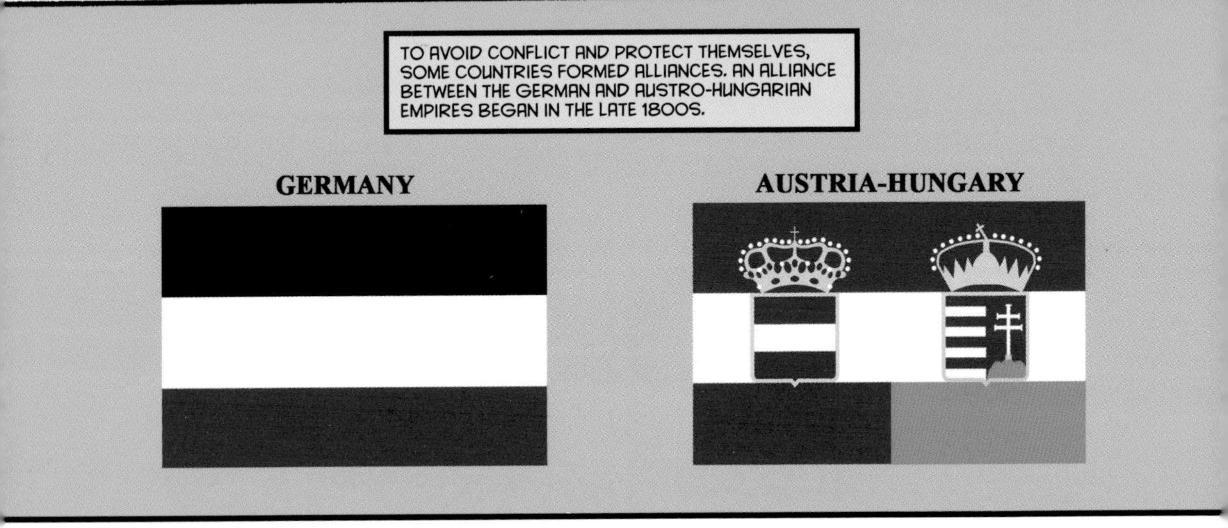
TO AVOID CONFLICT AND PROTECT THEMSELVES, SOME COUNTRIES FORMED ALLIANCES. AN ALLIANCE BETWEEN THE GERMAN AND AUSTRO-HUNGARIAN EMPIRES BEGAN IN THE LATE 1800S.
GERMANY
AUSTRIA-HUNGARY

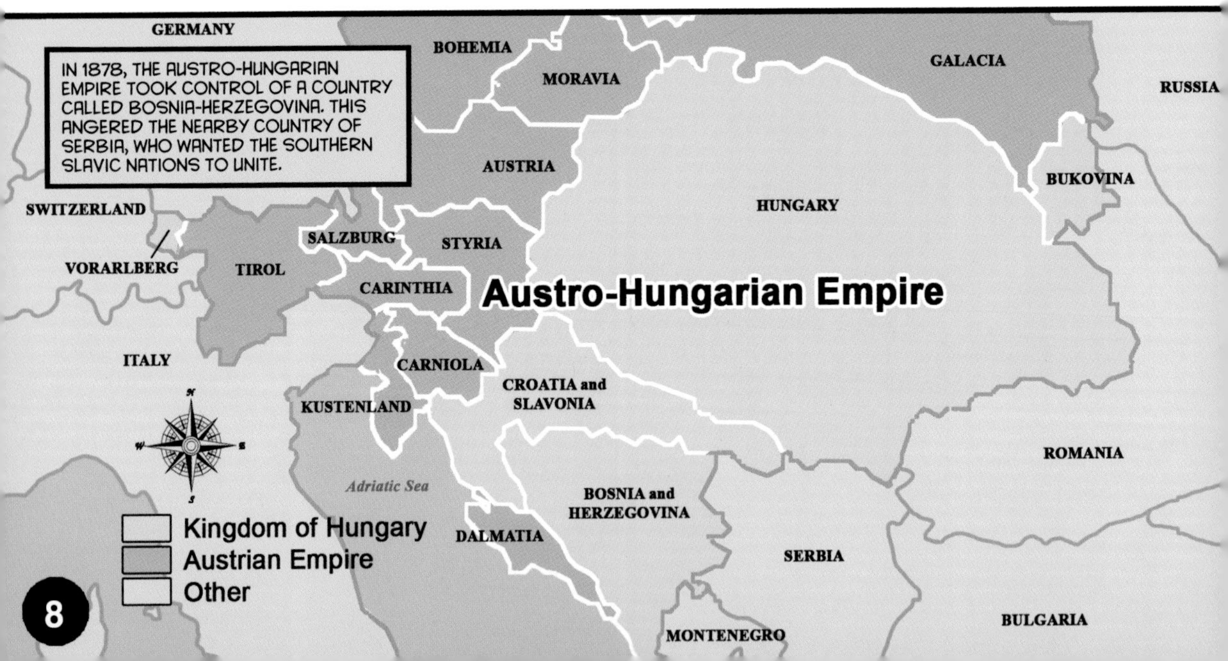
IN 1878, THE AUSTRO-HUNGARIAN EMPIRE TOOK CONTROL OF A COUNTRY CALLED BOSNIA-HERZEGOVINA. THIS ANGERED THE NEARBY COUNTRY OF SERBIA, WHO WANTED THE SOUTHERN SLAVIC NATIONS TO UNITE.
GERMANY
BOHEMIA
MORAVIA
GALACIA
RUSSIA
AUSTRIA
BUKOVINA
SWITZERLAND
HUNGARY
SALZBURG
STYRIA
VORARLBERG
TIROL
CARINTHIA
Austro-Hungarian Empire
ITALY
CARNIOLA
CROATIA and SLAVONIA
KUSTENLAND
ROMANIA
Adriatic Sea
BOSNIA and HERZEGOVINA
Kingdom of Hungary
Austrian Empire
Other
DALMATIA
SERBIA
BULGARIA
MONTENEGRO

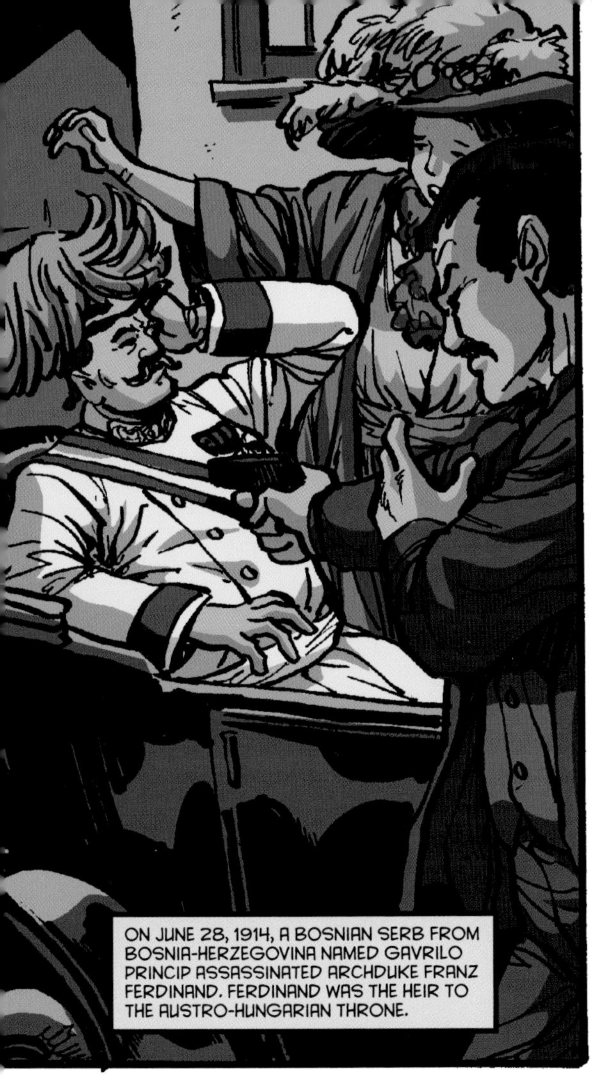
ON JUNE 28, 1914, A BOSNIAN SERB FROM BOSNIA-HERZEGOVINA NAMED GAVRILO PRINCIP ASSASSINATED ARCHDUKE FRANZ FERDINAND. FERDINAND WAS THE HEIR TO THE AUSTRO-HUNGARIAN THRONE.

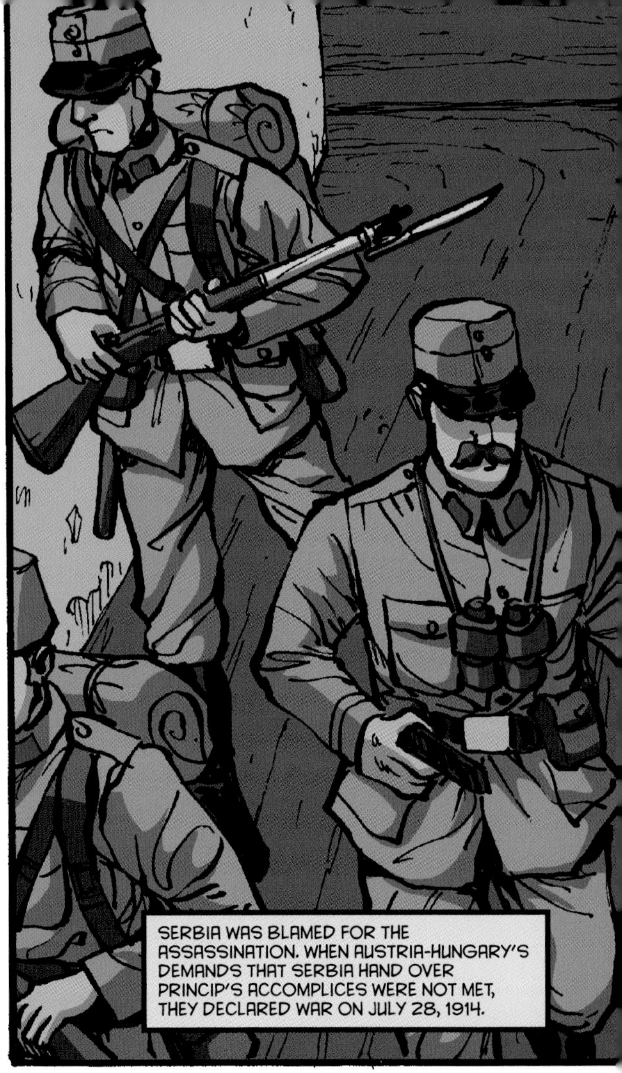
SERBIA WAS BLAMED FOR THE ASSASSINATION. WHEN AUSTRIA-HUNGARY'S DEMANDS THAT SERBIA HAND OVER PRINCIP'S ACCOMPLICES WERE NOT MET, THEY DECLARED WAR ON JULY 28, 1914.

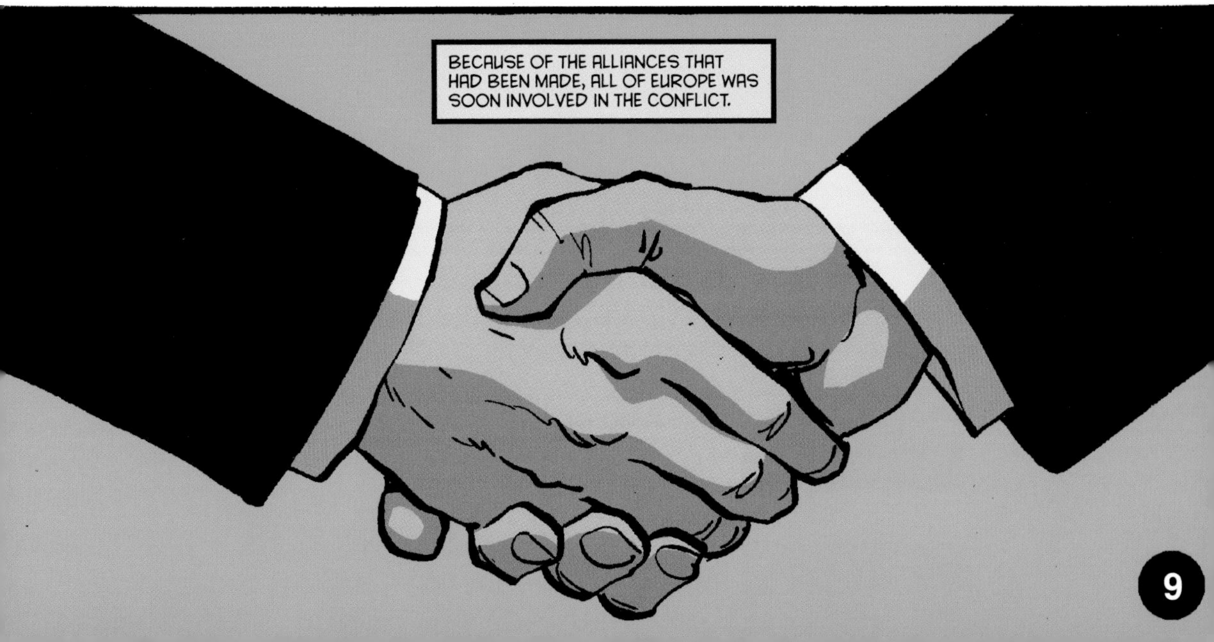
BECAUSE OF THE ALLIANCES THAT HAD BEEN MADE, ALL OF EUROPE WAS SOON INVOLVED IN THE CONFLICT.

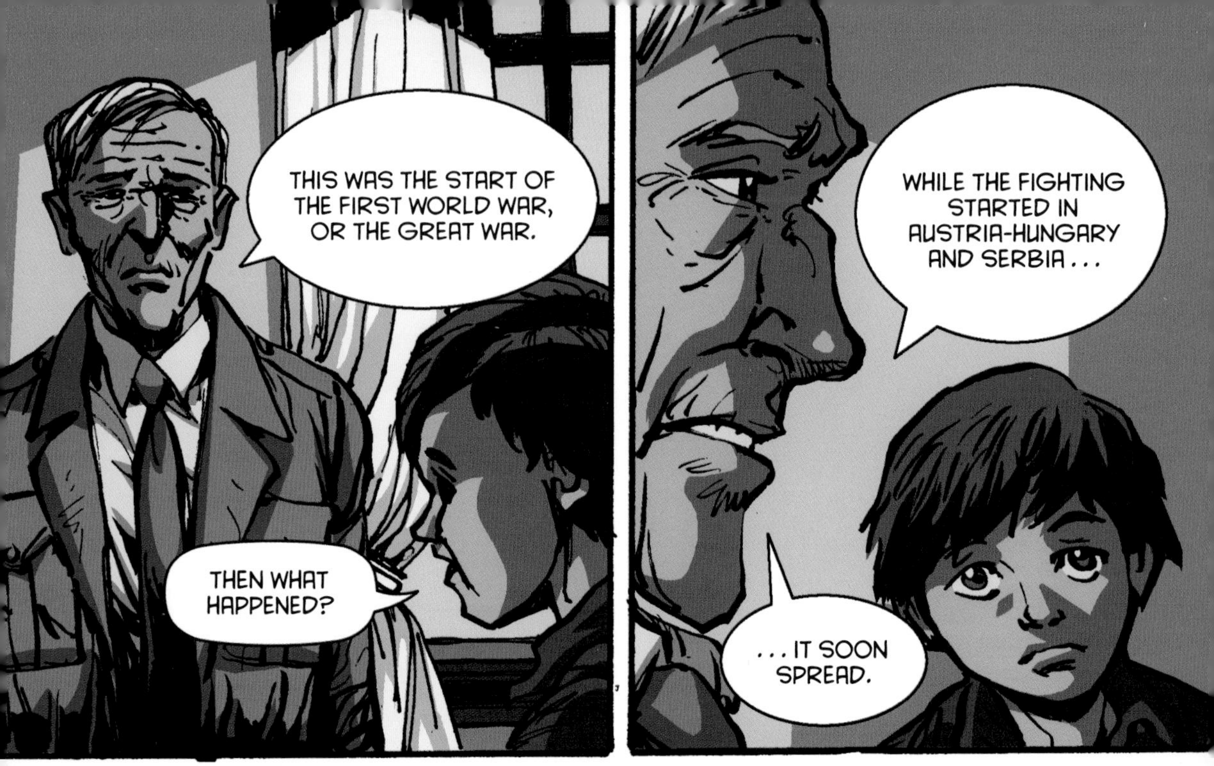
THIS WAS THE START OF THE FIRST WORLD WAR, OR THE GREAT WAR.
THEN WHAT HAPPENED?
WHILE THE FIGHTING STARTED IN AUSTRIA-HUNGARY AND SERBIA . . .
. . . IT SOON SPREAD.

MANY COUNTRIES FORMED THE ALLIED POWERS. THE MAIN MEMBERS WERE FRANCE, BRITAIN, RUSSIA, SERBIA, AND ITALY.

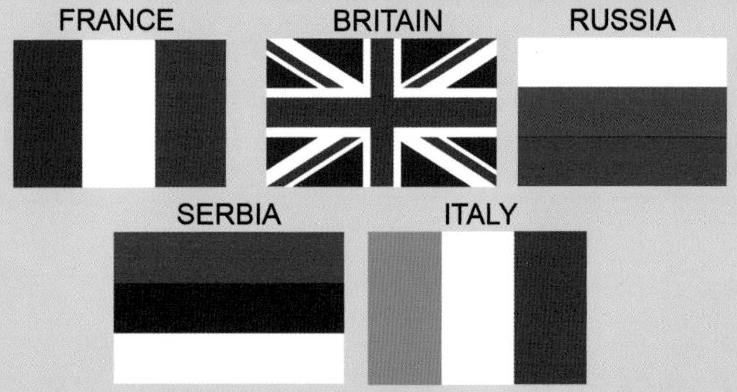
FRANCE
BRITAIN
RUSSIA
SERBIA
ITALY

MEANWHILE, THE CENTRAL POWERS WERE MADE UP OF THE GERMAN, AUSTRO-HUNGARIAN, AND OTTOMAN EMPIRES.

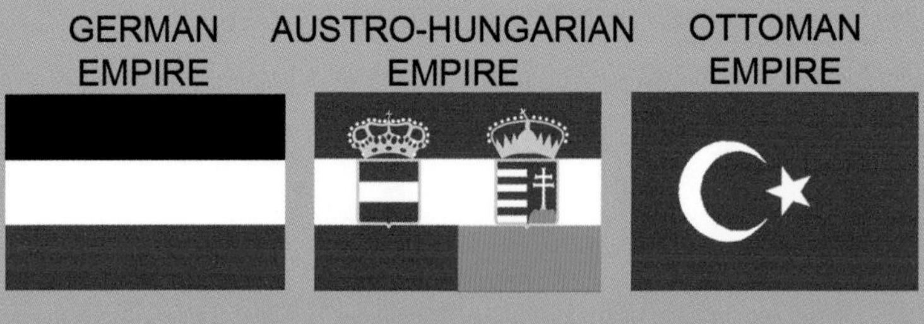
GERMAN EMPIRE
AUSTRO-HUNGARIAN EMPIRE
OTTOMAN EMPIRE

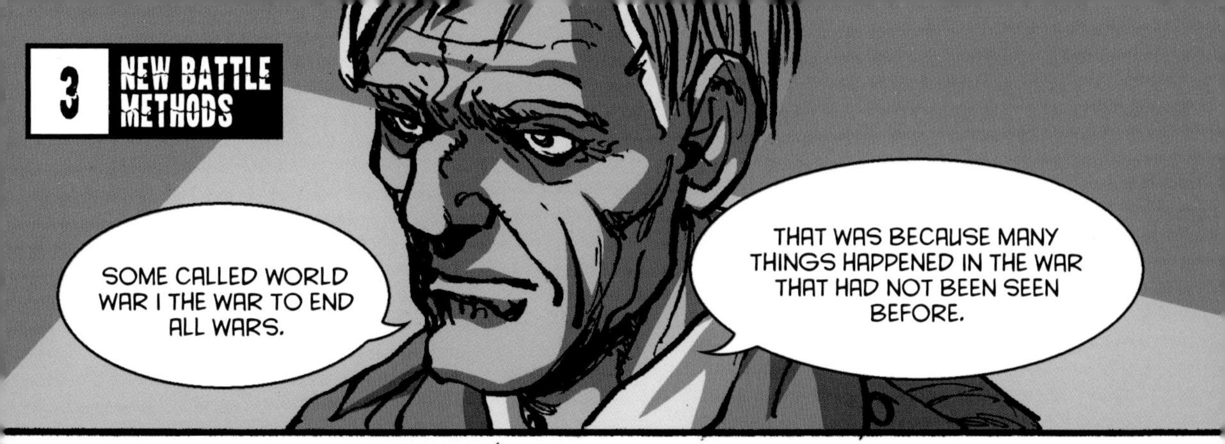
3 NEW BATTLE METHODS
SOME CALLED WORLD WAR I THE WAR TO END ALL WARS.
THAT WAS BECAUSE MANY THINGS HAPPENED IN THE WAR THAT HAD NOT BEEN SEEN BEFORE.

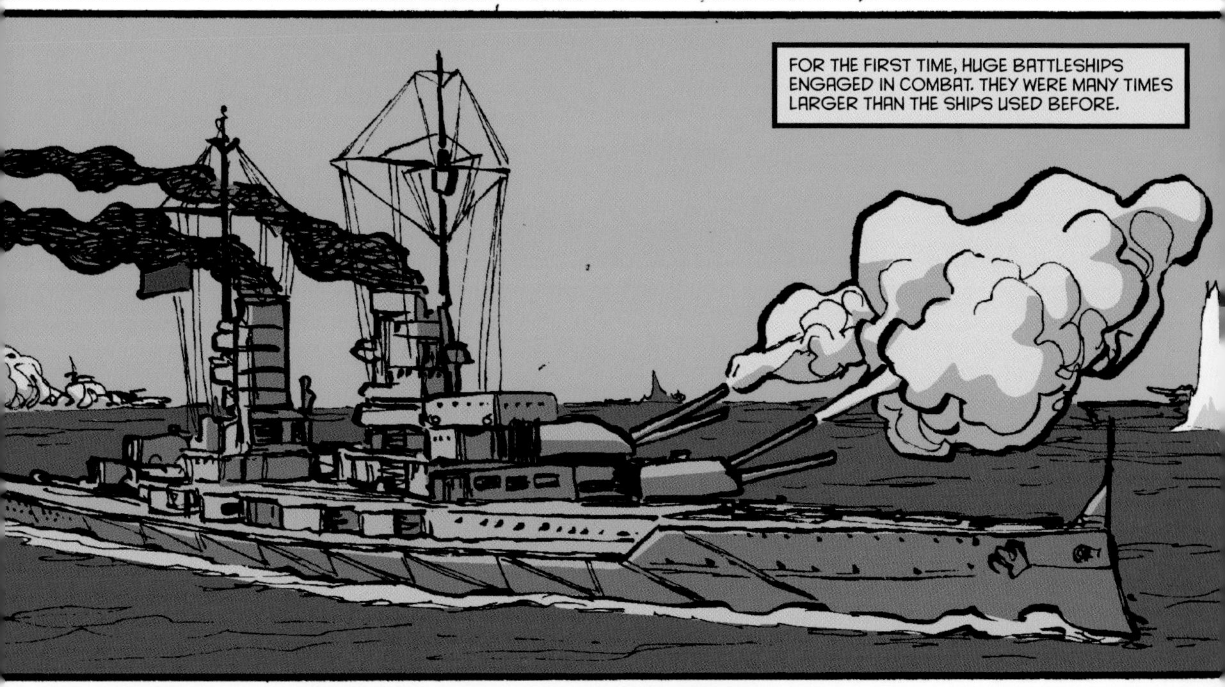
FOR THE FIRST TIME, HUGE BATTLESHIPS ENGAGED IN COMBAT. THEY WERE MANY TIMES LARGER THAN THE SHIPS USED BEFORE.

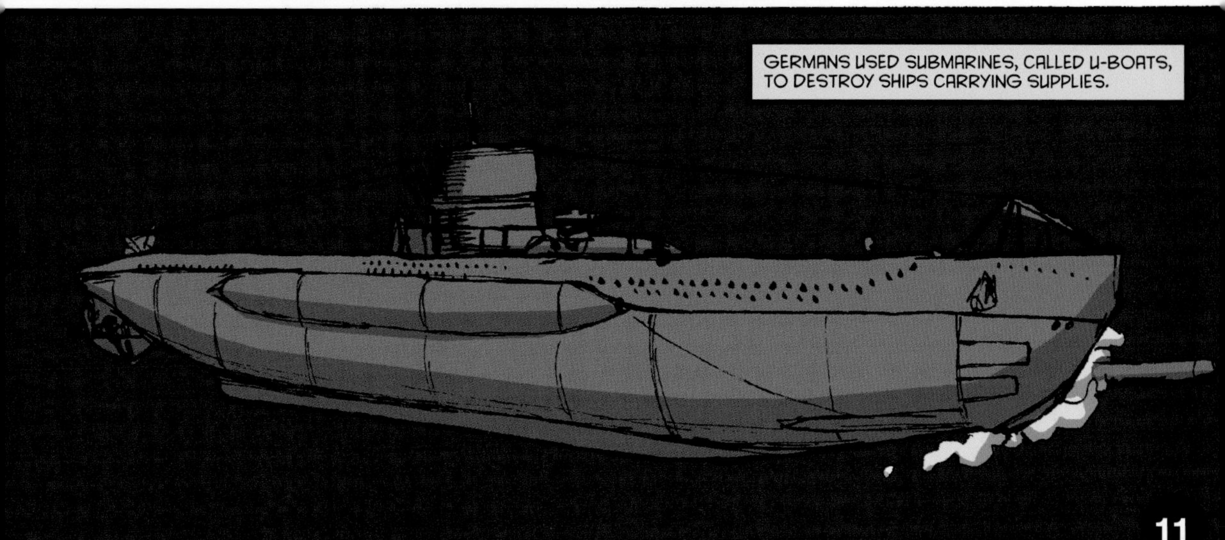
GERMANS USED SUBMARINES, CALLED U-BOATS, TO DESTROY SHIPS CARRYING SUPPLIES.

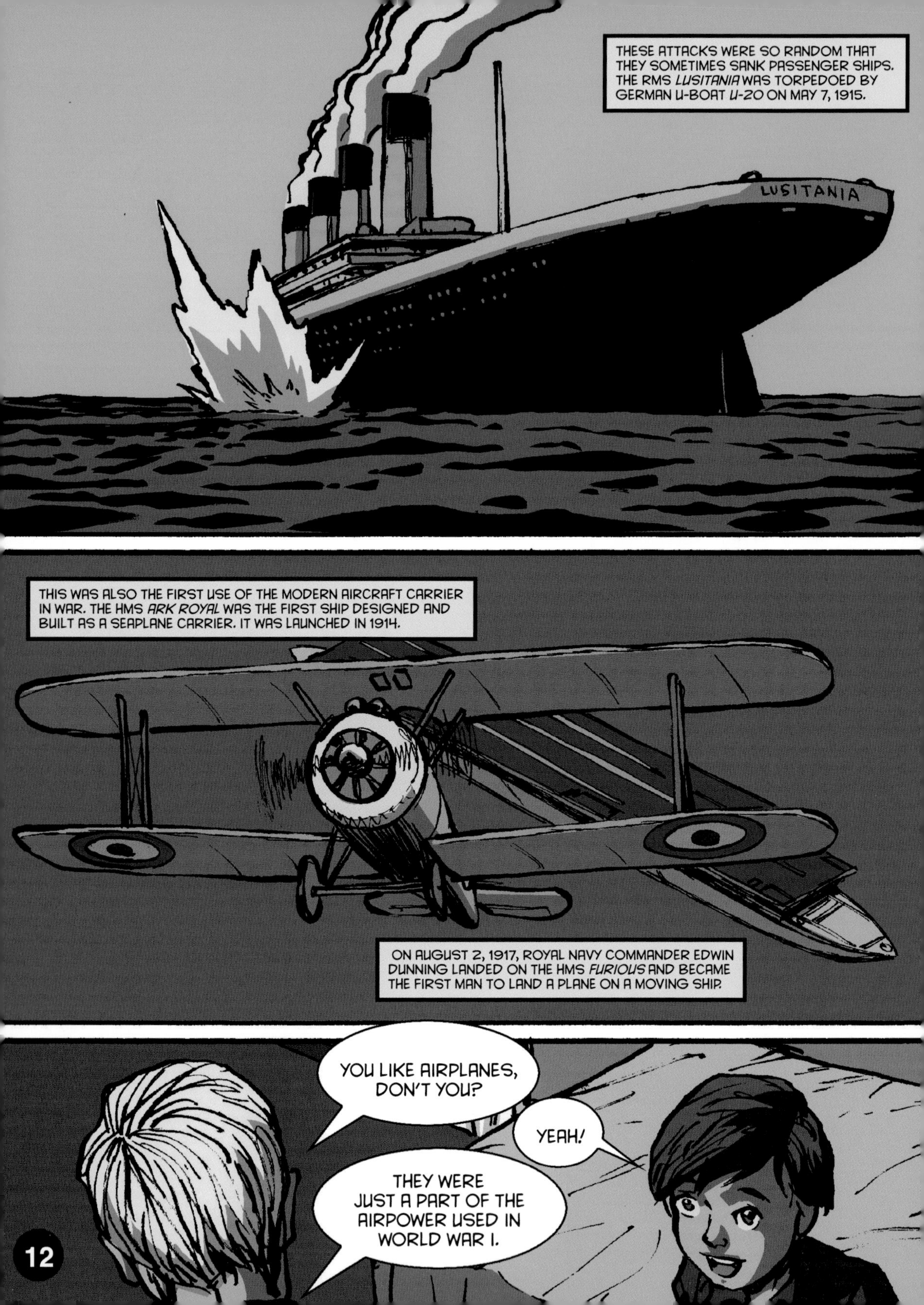
THESE ATTACKS WERE SO RANDOM THAT THEY SOMETIMES SANK PASSENGER SHIPS. THE RMS LUSITANIA WAS TORPEDOED BY GERMAN U-BOAT U-20 ON MAY 7, 1915.
LUSITANIA
THIS WAS ALSO THE FIRST USE OF THE MODERN AIRCRAFT CARRIER IN WAR. THE HMS ARK ROYAL WAS THE FIRST SHIP DESIGNED AND BUILT AS A SEAPLANE CARRIER. IT WAS LAUNCHED IN 1914.
ON AUGUST 2, 1917, ROYAL NAVY COMMANDER EDWIN DUNNING LANDED ON THE HMS FURIOUS AND BECAME THE FIRST MAN TO LAND A PLANE ON A MOVING SHIP.
YOU LIKE AIRPLANES, DON'T YOU?
YEAH!
THEY WERE JUST A PART OF THE AIRPOWER USED IN WORLD WAR I.

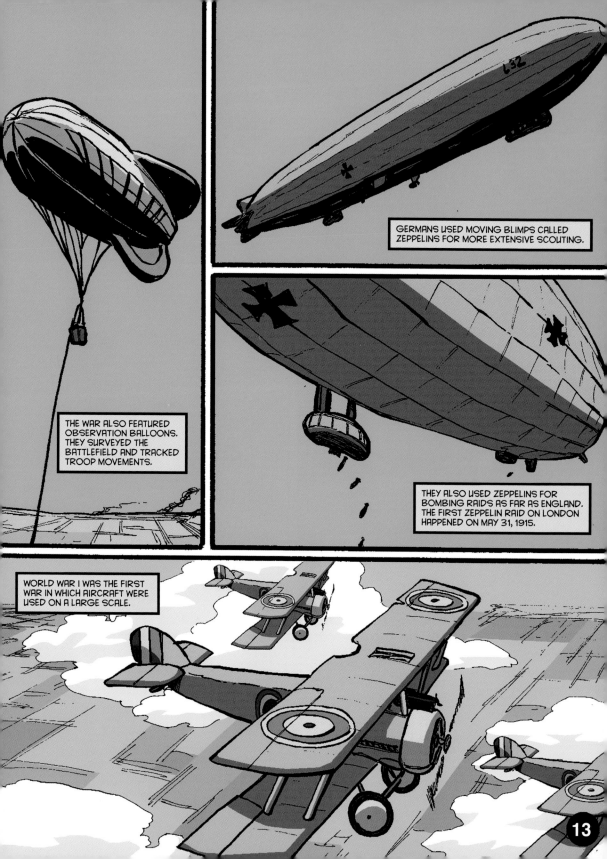

GERMANS USED MOVING BLIMPS CALLED ZEPPELINS FOR MORE EXTENSIVE SCOUTING.

THE WAR ALSO FEATURED OBSERVATION BALLOONS. THEY SURVEYED THE BATTLEFIELD AND TRACKED TROOP MOVEMENTS.

THEY ALSO USED ZEPPELINS FOR BOMBING RAIDS AS FAR AS ENGLAND. THE FIRST ZEPPELIN RAID ON LONDON HAPPENED ON MAY 31, 1915.

WORLD WAR I WAS THE FIRST WAR IN WHICH AIRCRAFT WERE USED ON A LARGE SCALE.

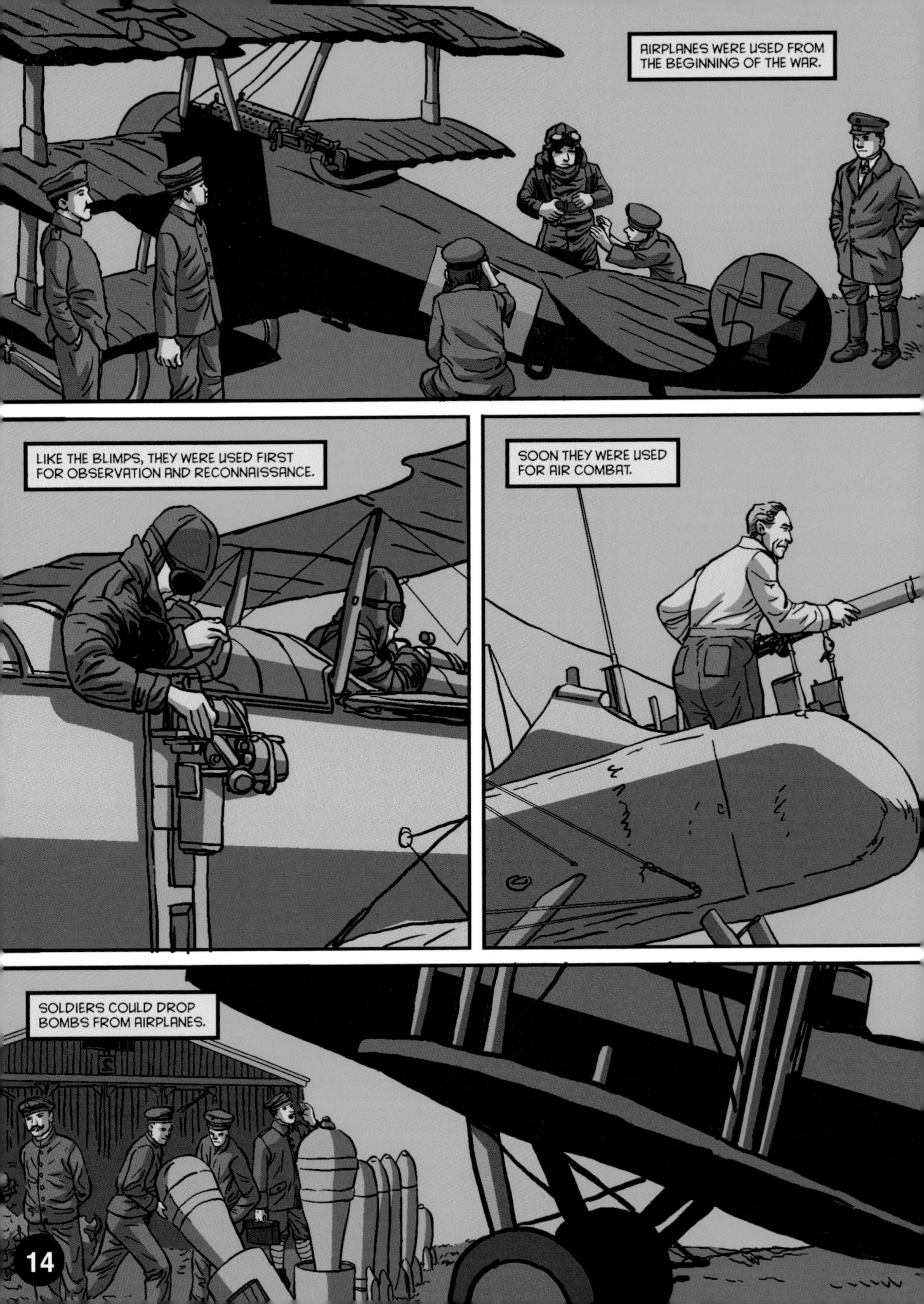
AIRPLANES WERE USED FROM THE BEGINNING OF THE WAR.
LIKE THE BLIMPS, THEY WERE USED FIRST FOR OBSERVATION AND RECONNAISSANCE.
SOON THEY WERE USED FOR AIR COMBAT.
SOLDIERS COULD DROP BOMBS FROM AIRPLANES.

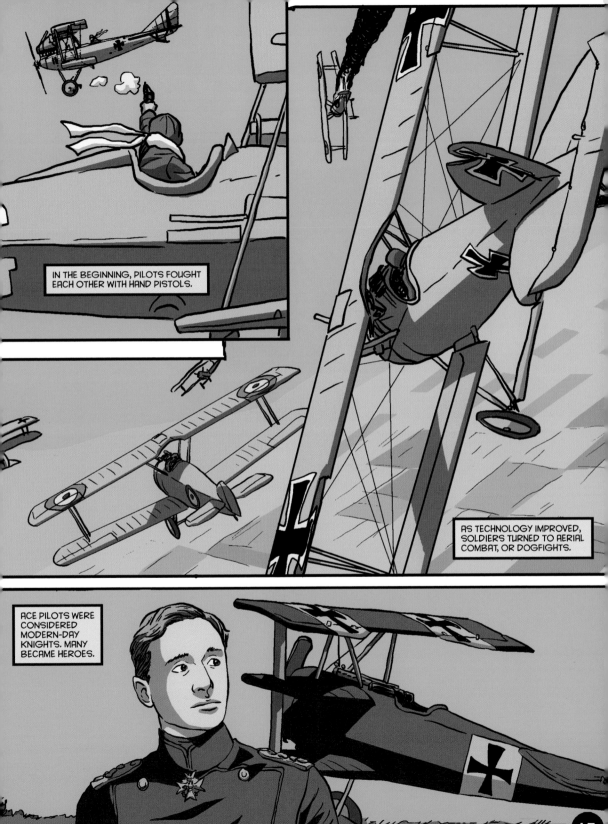

IN THE BEGINNING, PILOTS FOUGHT EACH OTHER WITH HAND PISTOLS.

AS TECHNOLOGY IMPROVED, SOLDIERS TURNED TO AERIAL COMBAT, OR DOGFIGHTS.

ACE PILOTS WERE CONSIDERED MODERN-DAY KNIGHTS. MANY BECAME HEROES.

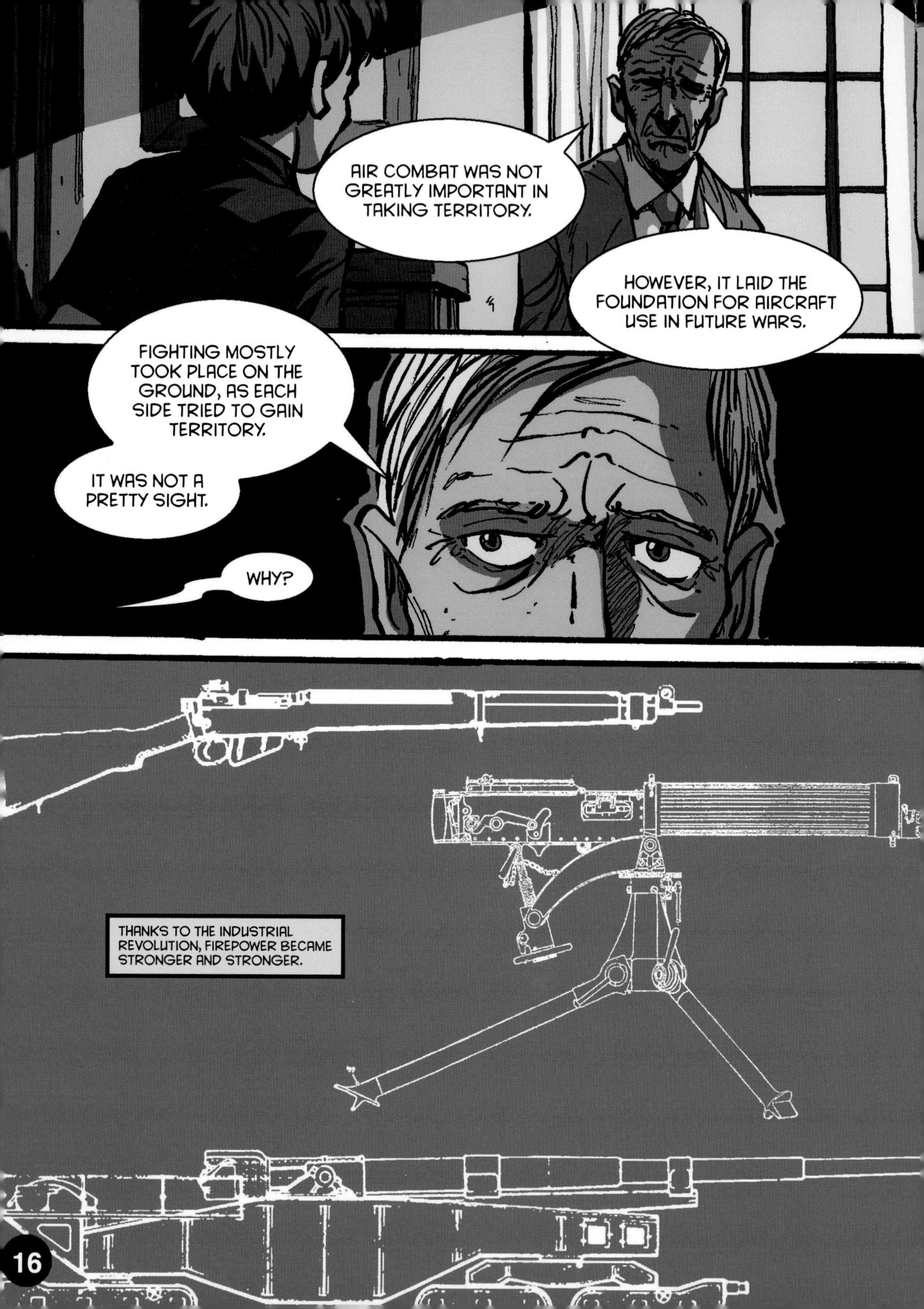
AIR COMBAT WAS NOT GREATLY IMPORTANT IN TAKING TERRITORY.
HOWEVER, IT LAID THE FOUNDATION FOR AIRCRAFT USE IN FUTURE WARS.
FIGHTING MOSTLY TOOK PLACE ON THE GROUND, AS EACH SIDE TRIED TO GAIN TERRITORY.
IT WAS NOT A PRETTY SIGHT.
WHY?
THANKS TO THE INDUSTRIAL REVOLUTION, FIREPOWER BECAME STRONGER AND STRONGER.

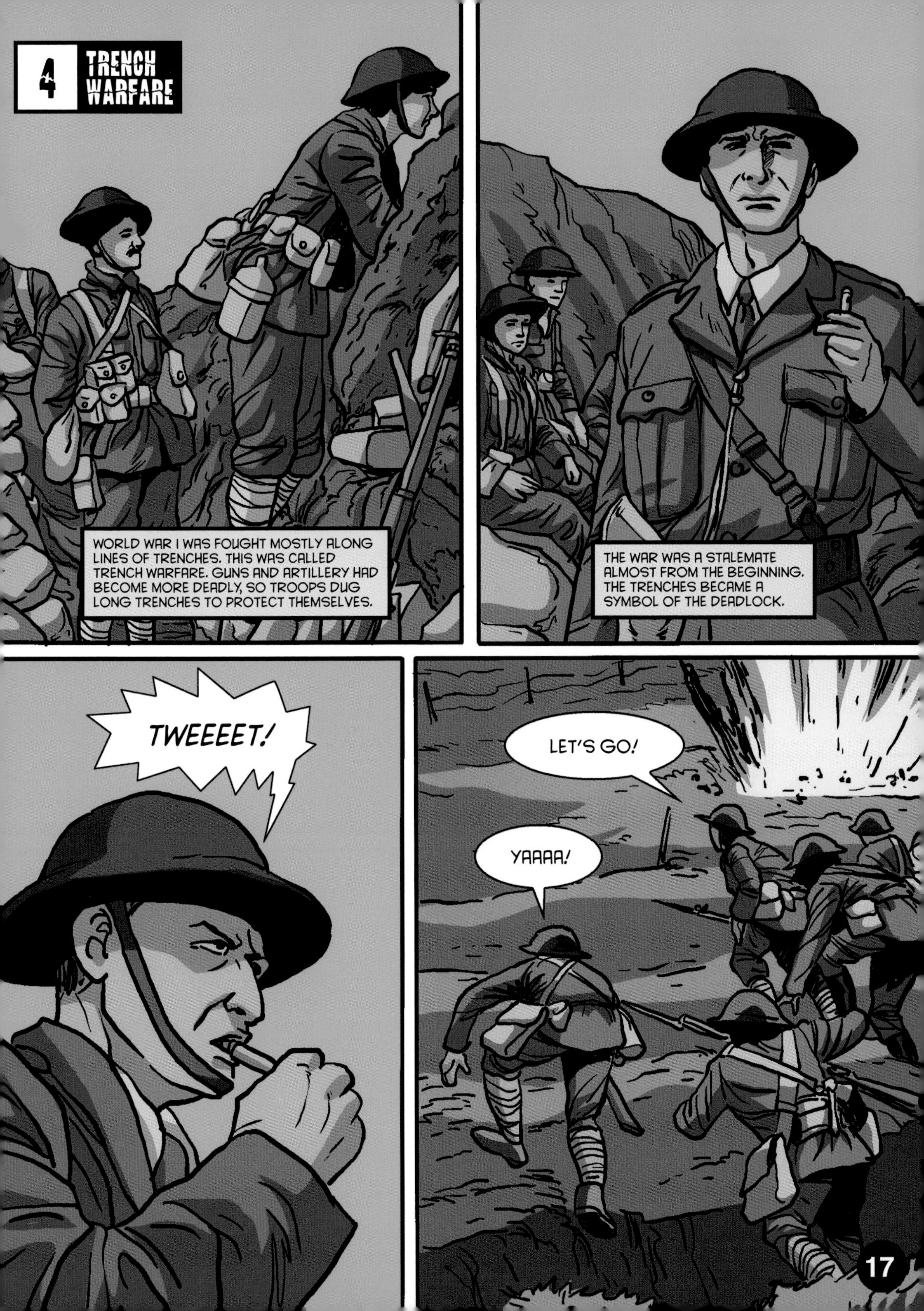
4 TRENCH WARFARE
WORLD WAR I WAS FOUGHT MOSTLY ALONG LINES OF TRENCHES. THIS WAS CALLED TRENCH WARFARE. GUNS AND ARTILLERY HAD BECOME MORE DEADLY, SO TROOPS DUG LONG TRENCHES TO PROTECT THEMSELVES.
THE WAR WAS A STALEMATE ALMOST FROM THE BEGINNING. THE TRENCHES BECAME A SYMBOL OF THE DEADLOCK.
TWEEEET!
LET'S GO!
YAAAA!

TRENCHES WERE A GREAT DEFENSIVE WEAPON. AN ATTACK BY EITHER SIDE WAS MET WITH A HAIL OF GUNFIRE AND ARTILLERY FIRE, CAUSING MASSIVE CASUALTIES.

EVEN IF AN ATTACK WAS SUCCESSFUL AT FIRST, THEY USUALLY COULD NOT SUSTAIN IT.

THIS WENT ON FOR MANY YEARS.

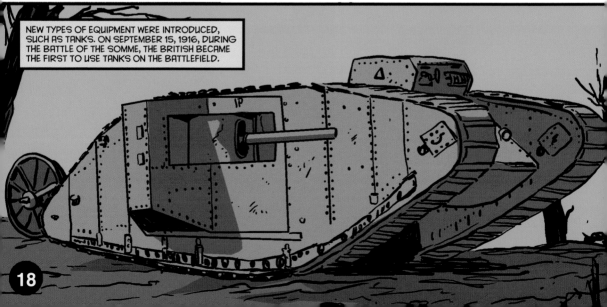

NEW TYPES OF EQUIPMENT WERE INTRODUCED, SUCH AS TANKS. ON SEPTEMBER 15, 1916, DURING THE BATTLE OF THE SOMME, THE BRITISH BECAME THE FIRST TO USE TANKS ON THE BATTLEFIELD.

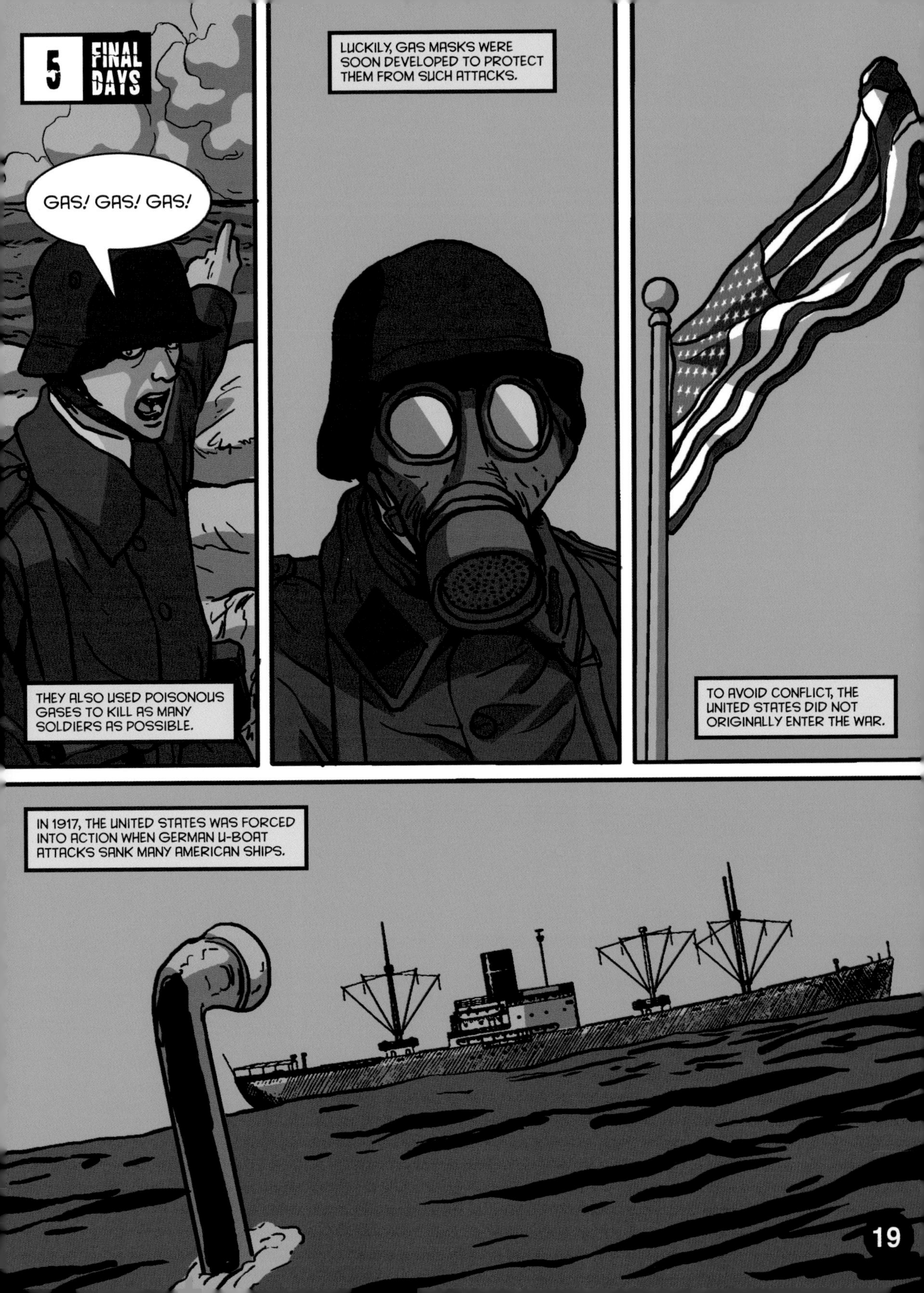
5 FINAL DAYS
GAS! GAS! GAS!
THEY ALSO USED POISONOUS GASES TO KILL AS MANY SOLDIERS AS POSSIBLE.
LUCKILY, GAS MASKS WERE SOON DEVELOPED TO PROTECT THEM FROM SUCH ATTACKS.
TO AVOID CONFLICT, THE UNITED STATES DID NOT ORIGINALLY ENTER THE WAR.
IN 1917, THE UNITED STATES WAS FORCED INTO ACTION WHEN GERMAN U-BOAT ATTACKS SANK MANY AMERICAN SHIPS.

ON JANUARY 19, 1917, THE UNITED STATES ENTERED THE WAR WHEN IT DECLARED WAR ON GERMANY. THIS SHIFTED THE BALANCE OF POWER TO THE ALLIES.

THE CENTRAL POWERS KNEW THEIR DEFEAT WAS NOW UNAVOIDABLE. SO THEY OFFERED THEIR SURRENDER.

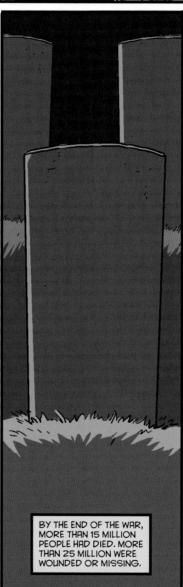

BY THE END OF THE WAR, MORE THAN 15 MILLION PEOPLE HAD DIED. MORE THAN 25 MILLION WERE WOUNDED OR MISSING.

BUT THE WAR WAS NOW OVER.

THE ARMISTICE AGREEMENT WAS OFFICIALLY MADE IN THE CITY OF COMPIÈGNE, FRANCE.

MARSHAL FERDINAND FOCH REPRESENTED THE ALLIES. MATTHIAS ERZBERGER REPRESENTED THE CENTRAL POWERS. THEY MET IN A RAILWAY CAR.

THEY SIGNED THE ARMISTICE TREATY IN THE EARLY MORNING HOURS OF NOVEMBER 11, 1918.

A COMPLETE CEASE-FIRE WAS AGREED UPON AT 11:00 A.M. ON THE ELEVENTH DAY OF NOVEMBER, THE ELEVENTH MONTH.

NOVEMBER 1918

	Monday	Tuesday	Wednesday	Thursday	
					1
4	5	6	7	8	9
11	12	13	14	15	16
18	19	20	21	22	23
25	26	27	28	29	30

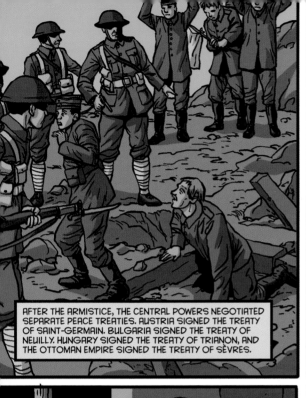

AFTER THE ARMISTICE, THE CENTRAL POWERS NEGOTIATED SEPARATE PEACE TREATIES. AUSTRIA SIGNED THE TREATY OF SAINT-GERMAIN. BULGARIA SIGNED THE TREATY OF NEUILLY. HUNGARY SIGNED THE TREATY OF TRIANON, AND THE OTTOMAN EMPIRE SIGNED THE TREATY OF SÈVRES.

THE ALLIES FORCED GERMANY TO ACCEPT SOLE RESPONSIBILITY FOR THE WAR. AFTER SIGNING THE TREATY OF VERSAILLES, GERMANY HAD TO GIVE UP LARGE AMOUNTS OF LAND AND DISMANTLE ITS MILITARY. IT ALSO HAD TO AGREE TO PAY REPARATIONS TO AFFECTED COUNTRIES.

THIS LED TO POVERTY AND OTHER ECONOMIC PROBLEMS IN GERMANY.

MANY BELIEVE THIS LED TO THE RISE IN POWER OF NAZI GERMANY AND ADOLF HITLER. THOSE EVENTS WOULD SEND THE WORLD INTO THE SECOND WORLD WAR.

7 ARMISTICE DAY AROUND THE WORLD

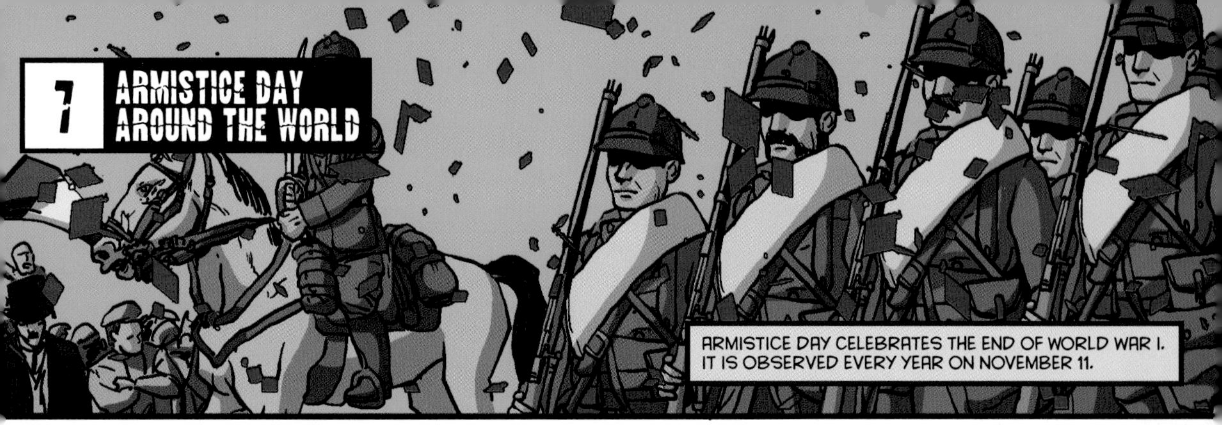
ARMISTICE DAY CELEBRATES THE END OF WORLD WAR I. IT IS OBSERVED EVERY YEAR ON NOVEMBER 11.

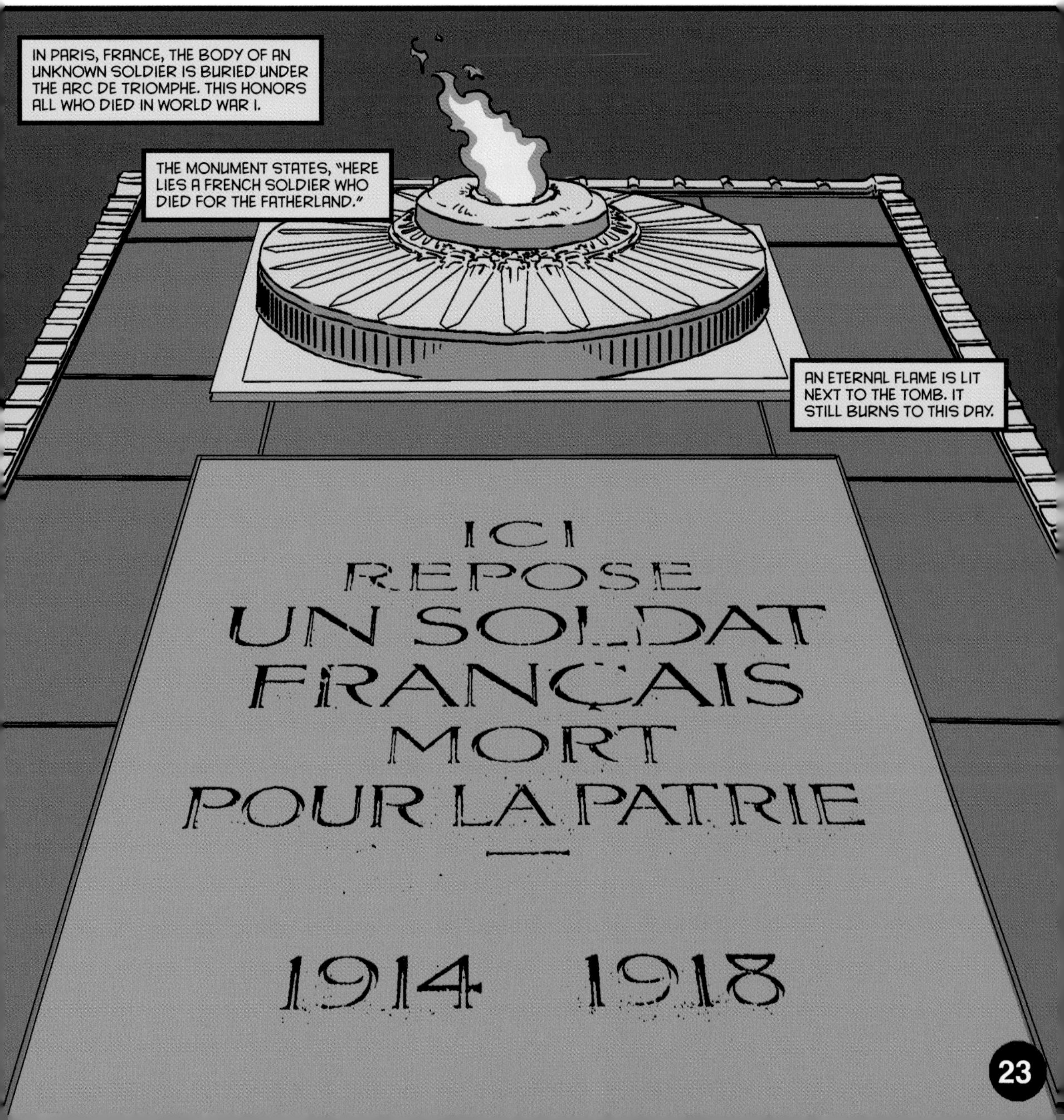
IN PARIS, FRANCE, THE BODY OF AN UNKNOWN SOLDIER IS BURIED UNDER THE ARC DE TRIOMPHE. THIS HONORS ALL WHO DIED IN WORLD WAR I.
THE MONUMENT STATES, "HERE LIES A FRENCH SOLDIER WHO DIED FOR THE FATHERLAND."
AN ETERNAL FLAME IS LIT NEXT TO THE TOMB. IT STILL BURNS TO THIS DAY.
ICI REPOSE UN SOLDAT FRANÇAIS MORT POUR LA PATRIE
1914 1918

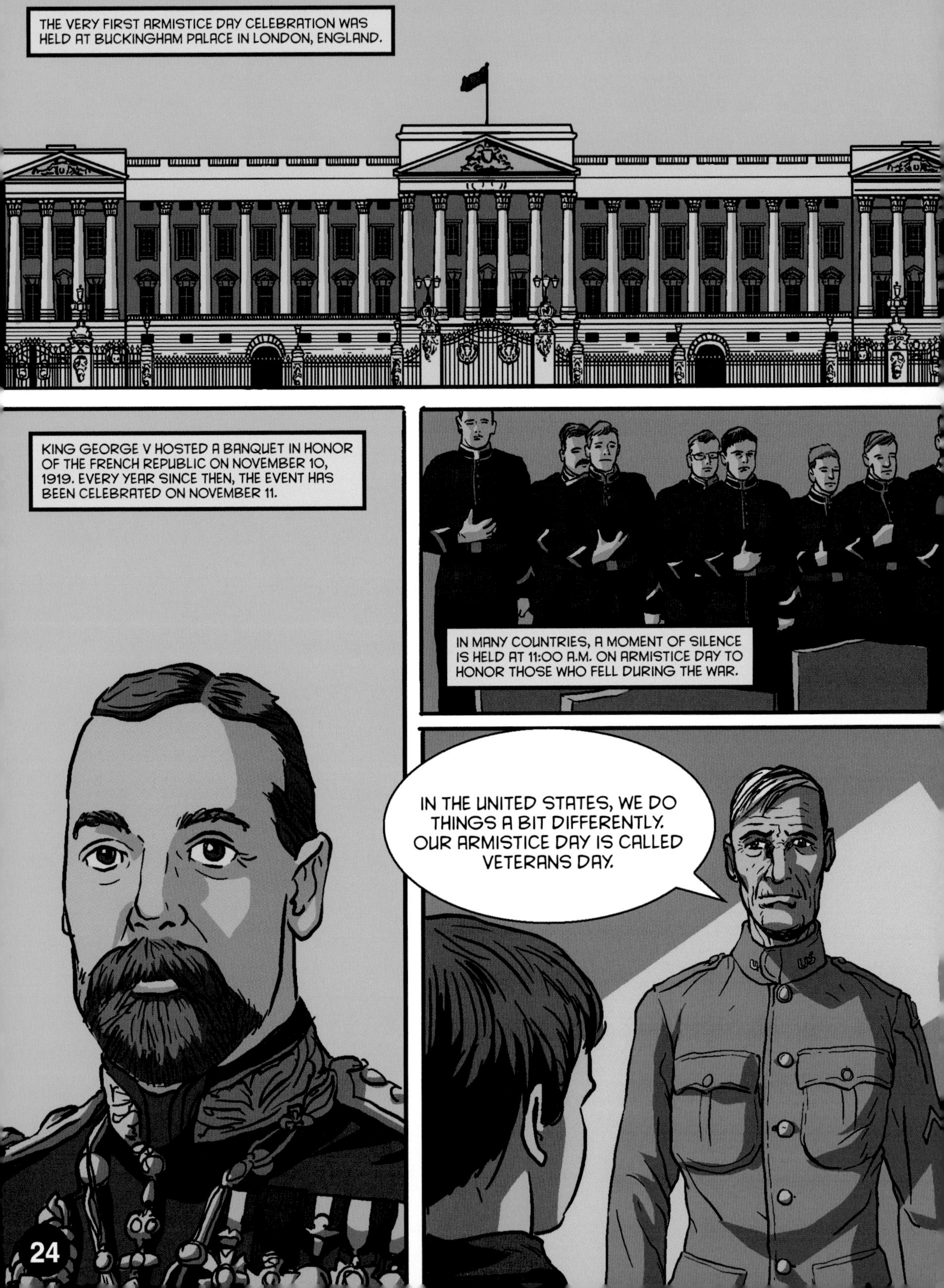
THE VERY FIRST ARMISTICE DAY CELEBRATION WAS HELD AT BUCKINGHAM PALACE IN LONDON, ENGLAND.
KING GEORGE V HOSTED A BANQUET IN HONOR OF THE FRENCH REPUBLIC ON NOVEMBER 10, 1919. EVERY YEAR SINCE THEN, THE EVENT HAS BEEN CELEBRATED ON NOVEMBER 11.
IN MANY COUNTRIES, A MOMENT OF SILENCE IS HELD AT 11:00 A.M. ON ARMISTICE DAY TO HONOR THOSE WHO FELL DURING THE WAR.
IN THE UNITED STATES, WE DO THINGS A BIT DIFFERENTLY. OUR ARMISTICE DAY IS CALLED VETERANS DAY.

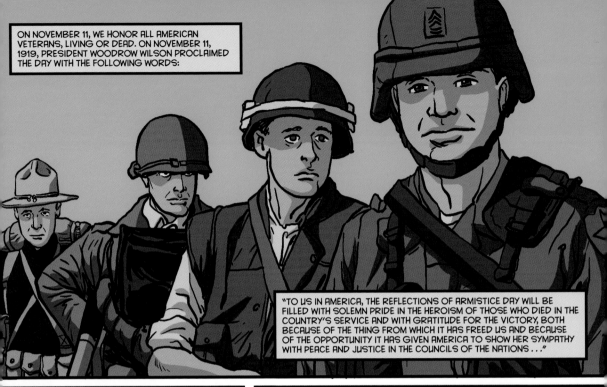

ON NOVEMBER 11, WE HONOR ALL AMERICAN VETERANS, LIVING OR DEAD. ON NOVEMBER 11, 1919, PRESIDENT WOODROW WILSON PROCLAIMED THE DAY WITH THE FOLLOWING WORDS:

"TO US IN AMERICA, THE REFLECTIONS OF ARMISTICE DAY WILL BE FILLED WITH SOLEMN PRIDE IN THE HEROISM OF THOSE WHO DIED IN THE COUNTRY'S SERVICE AND WITH GRATITUDE FOR THE VICTORY, BOTH BECAUSE OF THE THING FROM WHICH IT HAS FREED US AND BECAUSE OF THE OPPORTUNITY IT HAS GIVEN AMERICA TO SHOW HER SYMPATHY WITH PEACE AND JUSTICE IN THE COUNCILS OF THE NATIONS . . ."

TODAY IS VETERANS DAY. FOR SOME, IT'S ARMISTICE DAY. I AM CELEBRATING THAT DAY.

THANK YOU, GRANDPA!

HONORING THOSE WHO SERVED, HONORED, AND LOVED THEIR COUNTRY.

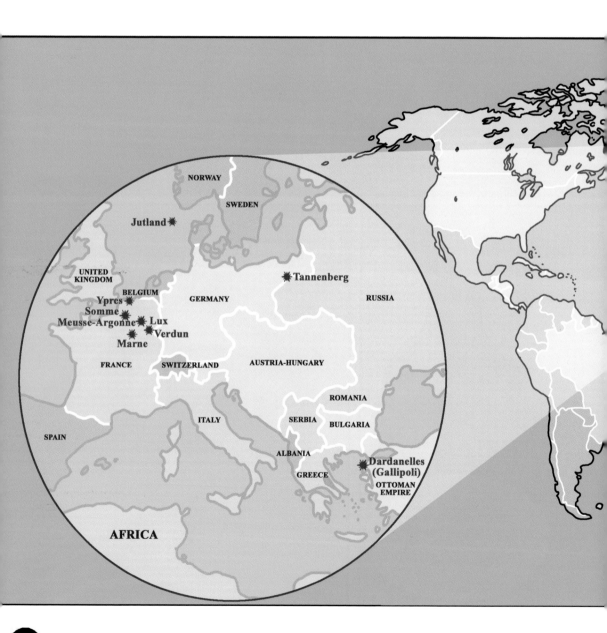

NORWAY

SWEDEN

Jutland ✳

UNITED
KINGDOM

BELGIUM

Ypres ✳
Somme ✳
Meusse-Argonne ✳ ✳ Lux
✳ ✳ Verdun
Marne

FRANCE   SWITZERLAND

SPAIN

ITALY

AFRICA

GERMANY

✳ Tannenberg

RUSSIA

AUSTRIA-HUNGARY

ROMANIA

SERBIA   BULGARIA

ALBANIA

GREECE

✳ Dardanelles
(Gallipoli)

OTTOMAN
EMPIRE

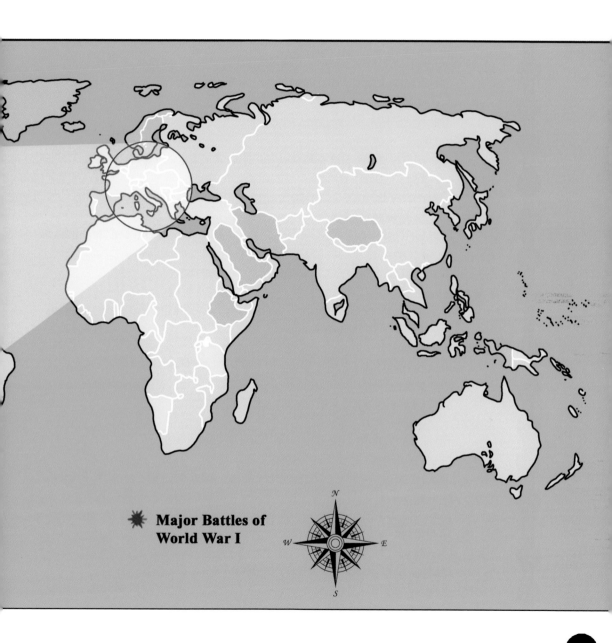

☀ **Major Battles of World War I**

1914 June 28
    Gavrilo Princip assassinated Archduke Franz Ferdinand, nephew of Franz Joseph and heir to the Austro-Hungarian throne, and Ferdinand's wife, Sophie.

1914 July 28
    Austria-Hungary declared war on Serbia.

1914 September
    The HMS *Ark Royal* was launched.

1915 May 7
    Germany sank the passenger ship RMS *Lusitania*.

1915 May 31
    Germany bombed London, England, with Zeppelins for the first time.

1916 September 15
    The British became the first to use tanks on the battlefield.

1917 January 19
    The United States declared war on Germany.

1917 August 2
    Royal Navy commander Edwin Dunning landed his plane on the moving HMS *Furious*.

1918 November 11
    The Armistice of Compiègne went into effect at 11:00 a.m.

1919 June 28
    Germany signed the Treaty of Versailles.

1919 September 10
    Austria signed the Treaty of Saint-Germain.

1919 November 10
    The first Armistice Day celebration was held in London, England.

1919 November 11
    President Woodrow Wilson proclaimed November 11 as Armistice Day in the United States.

1919 November 27
    Bulgaria signed the Treaty of Neuilly.

1920 June 4
    Hungary signed the Treaty of Trianon.

1920 August 10
    The Ottoman Empire signed the Treaty of Sèvres.

BIOGRAPHIES

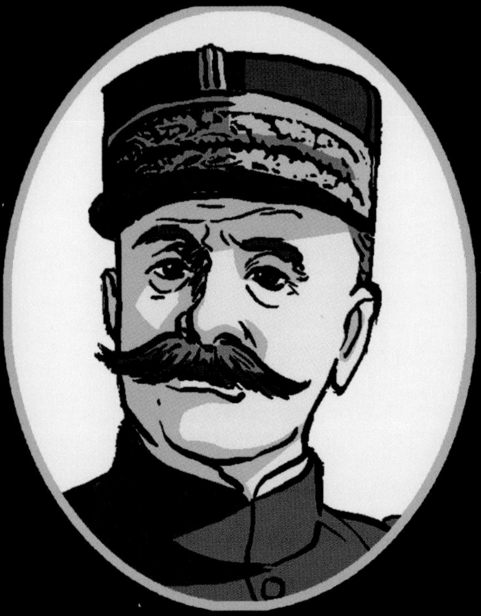

FERDINAND FOCH

(October 2, 1851–March 20, 1929)

Marshal Ferdinand Foch was a commander in the French army during World War I. In 1914, he was given command of troops on France's northern border with Germany. He successfully repelled German advancement at the First Battle of the Marne and the Battles of Ypres. In 1918, he was named supreme commander of Allied forces. By August of that year, Foch's forces had driven the Germans back, and Germany was forced to request an armistice. Foch dictated the terms of the November 1918 armistice. He died March 20, 1929, in Paris, France.

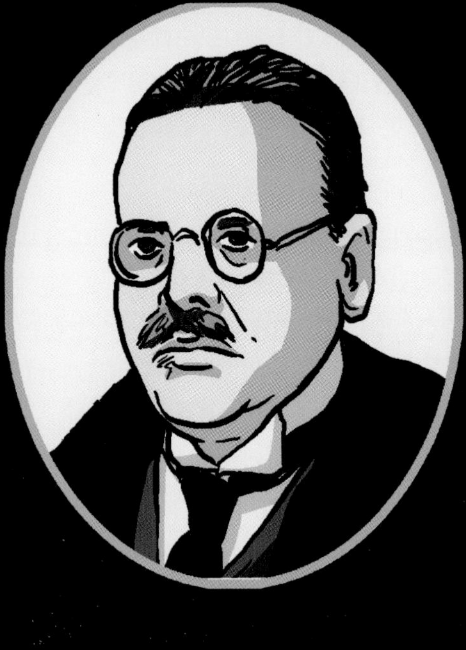

MATTHIAS ERZBERGER

(September 20, 1875–August 26, 1921)

Matthias Erzberger was a Centre Party member who was elected to the German Parliament, called the Reichstag, in 1903. He was an early supporter of Germany's participation in World War I. Later, he was a supporter of a negotiated peace. On November 11, 1918, Erzberger led the German delegation and signed the armistice in Compiègne, France. In 1919, he became Germany's finance minister. In 1920, Adolf Hitler and the National Socialist movement rose to power. Erzberger was forced from office. He was assassinated by nationalist forces on August 26, 1921.

QUICK STATS

World War I

Dates: 1914–1918

Number of Casualties:

For the Allies:
20,855,804

For the Central
powers: 15,036,422

Belligerents:

The Allied powers:
Russia, British Empire, France, Italy, United States, Japan, Romania, Serbia, Belgium, Greece, Portugal, Montenegro

The Central powers:
Germany, Austria-Hungary, Ottoman Empire, Bulgaria

Important Leaders:

For the Allied powers:
US president Woodrow Wilson, French premier Georges Clemenceau, British prime minister David Lloyd George, Italian prime minister Vittorio Orlando

For the Central powers:
German kaiser Wilhelm II, Emperor of Austria and King of Hungary Franz Joseph I, Ottoman Empire pashas Mehmed Talaat, Ismail Enver, and Ahmed Djemal, Bulgarian tsar Ferdinand I

GLOSSARY

abdicate
to give up power.

alliance
a relationship in which people agree to work together.

allies
people, groups, or nations united for some special purpose.

armistice
an agreement to stop fighting.

artillery
a branch of the military armed with large firearms, such as cannons or rockets.

assassinate
to murder a very important person, usually for political reasons.

casualty
a person lost through death, wounds, or capture due to war or an accident.

cease-fire
a temporary stopping of hostile activities.

commemorate
something that exists or is done in order to remind people of an important person or event from the past.

deadlock
a situation in which an agreement cannot be made.

dismantle
to take something such as a machine or a structure apart so that it is in separate pieces.

economic
relating to the production and use of goods and services.

Industrial Revolution
the period in the 1800s when new machinery and technology changed the world economy.

Nazi
a member of the German political party that controlled Germany under Adolf Hitler.

negotiate
to work out an agreement about the terms of something.

reconnaissance
an inspection the military uses to gain information about enemy territory.

reparation
money that a country or group that loses a war pays because of the damage and deaths it caused.

stalemate
a condition in which neither side can win.

sustain
to provide what is needed in order for something to continue to exist.

WEBSITES

To learn more about Graphic Warfare, visit booklinks.abdopublishing.com. These links are routinely monitored and updated to provide the most current information available.